CH. PERRAULT

Little Red Riding Hood

Illustration: José M. Lavarello
Adaptation: Eduard José

Retold by Jane Belk Moncure

The Child's World, Inc.

Once upon a time, in a cottage in the woods, a kind and beautiful little girl lived with her parents.

One year, on the little girl's birthday, her parents gave her a red velvet cloak with a little red hood. The little girl danced, for she loved her beautiful new cloak. She wore it everywhere she went, and everyone called her Little Red Riding Hood.

Little Red Riding Hood's family was a happy one. Her father was a woodcutter, and though he did not make a great deal of money, he made enough to keep his family comfortable.

One day Little Red Riding Hood's father and another woodcutter were chopping logs when they saw something strange run through the forest.

"What was that?" asked the first woodcutter.

"It looked like a wolf," said Little Red Riding Hood's father. "We'd better be on the lookout for him. Those wolves can be crafty creatures."

One day shortly after that, Little Red Riding Hood's mother said to her, "Take these fresh buns and this jar of blackberry jam to your grandmother. She loves jam and will be happy to know we are thinking of her. But stay on the main path. Don't wander off it! Your father thinks there may be a wolf prowling about in the woods."

"I promise I will," said Little Red Riding Hood. She was happy for the chance to wear her pretty red cloak.

Soon Little Red Riding Hood was on her way. She skipped happily along the path, looking at the pretty flowers.

She thought to herself, "Grandmother would be happy if I took her some flowers."

So, she forgot her promise and left the path, looking for flowers to pick. Soon, without thinking, she had wandered deep into the woods, where the hungry wolf hid behind a tree. He licked his chops as he watched the girl coming closer.

Then, when she was very close, the wolf jumped onto the path right in front of her.

"Good morning, little girl," said the wolf. "Where are you going on this fine day?"

Now, Little Red Riding Hood had never seen a wolf before, so she was not afraid. She just thought the stranger was a little hairier than most people.

"I am going to Grandmother's house," she said.

"And where does your grandmother live?" asked the wicked wolf.

"She lives in the first cottage on the other side of the woods," said Little Red Riding Hood.

The wolf thought to himself, "What a fine meal they will both make!" So he said, "I have an idea. Let's play a game!"

"Oh, I love games!" said Little Red Riding Hood.

"Good," said the wolf. "Now, I'll take the long path and you take the short path. Let's see who gets there first."

Of course, the sneaky wolf had a trick up his sleeve. First he showed Little Red Riding Hood the long path. Then he raced off down the short path to Grandmother's house. He arrived there in no time and knocked on her door.

"Who is there?" asked Grandmother.

"Little Red Riding Hood," said the wolf in a high voice.

Grandmother got out of bed and went to the door. But no sooner had she lifted the latch than the wolf sprang through the door. He grabbed Grandmother and locked her in the cupboard. He wanted to eat her right up, but he knew that Little Red Riding Hood was on her way.

Quickly, the wolf put on Grandmother's night cap, hopped into her bed, and pulled up the covers.

Just then, Little Red Riding Hood knocked on the door.

"Who is there?" asked the big wolf in a high voice.

"It's your granddaughter," said Little Red
Riding Hood.
"Come in, come in. The door is open," said
the wolf.

Now it was dark inside the cottage and Little Red Riding Hood could not see very well. But even so, she thought her grandmother looked strange indeed. So she said, "Grandmother, what big ears you have!"

"The better to hear you with, my dear," said the wolf.

"But Grandmother, what big eyes you have!"

"The better to see you with, my dear."

"But Grandmother, what big hands you have!"

"The better to hold you with, my dear."

Then Little Red Riding Hood noticed the wolf's huge mouth and teeth. She leaned closer for a better look.

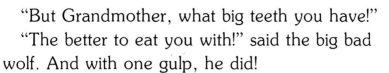

"But Grandmother, what big teeth you have!"

"The better to eat you with!" said the big bad wolf. And with one gulp, he did!

Now the wolf's belly was so full, he had no room for Grandmother. So he left the cottage and ran back into the woods.

A short time later, Little Red Riding Hood's father happened to pass by Grandmother's cottage. He decided to stop in to say hello. At first he thought that no one was home, but then he heard sounds coming from the cupboard. Imagine his shock when he opened it and found Grandmother!

"It's terrible! Just terrible!" she cried. "The wolf has gobbled up Little Red Riding Hood!"

The woodcutter's heart was filled with rage.

"This will be the last evil deed that wolf ever does!" he cried. His eyes were filled with tears as he grabbed his axe and went looking for the wolf.

In a short time, he found the wicked wolf asleep under a tree. The woodcutter lifted his axe and was just about to chop off the wolf's head when he heard a little voice say, "Help! Get me out of here!"

It was Little Red Riding Hood's voice. She was alive! The woodcutter was overjoyed. Carefully, he opened the wolf's tummy with his sharp axe. The wolf was so sleepy after his big meal that he didn't even wake up!

Out jumped Little Red Riding Hood, safe and sound.

"Oh Daddy! I've been so scared," cried the little girl.

"Now we will fix that wolf once and for all," said the woodcutter. "Help me find some rocks."

Then he carefully put the heavy rocks in the wolf's tummy and quickly sewed him up again.

An hour or two later, the wolf awoke and tried to stand up.

"Ooooh, my stomach," said the wolf. "That little girl was heavier than I thought. I need a drink of water."

Slowly, the wolf made his way to the river. Once there, he bent down to drink. But no sooner had he bent down, than the heavy stones tipped him over, and he sank quickly to the bottom of the river.

That was the end of the big bad wolf. Now the woods were safe. Children were free to pick flowers without fear. And from that day on, Little Red Riding Hood knew how to tell a wolf when she saw one.